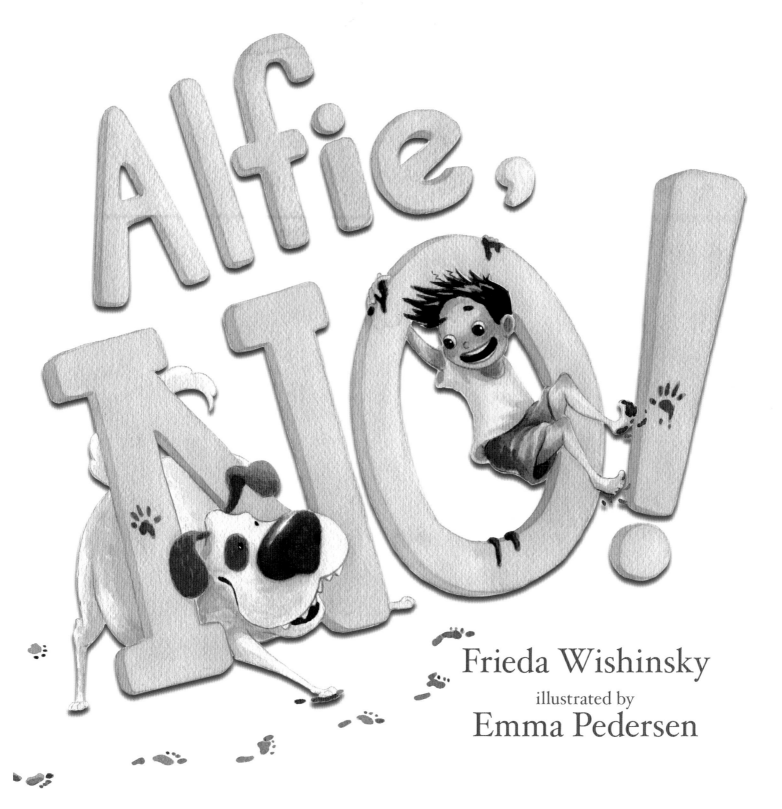

Alfie, NO!

Frieda Wishinsky

illustrated by
Emma Pedersen

North Winds Press
An Imprint of Scholastic Canada Ltd.

The art for this book was painted in gouache on Arches cold pressed watercolour paper.

Library and Archives Canada Cataloguing in Publication

Title: Alfie, no! / Frieda Wishinsky ; illustrations by Emma Pedersen.
Names: Wishinsky, Frieda, author. | Pedersen, Emma, 1988- illustrator
Description: Published simultaneously in softcover by Scholastic Canada Ltd.
Identifiers: Canadiana 20190065362 | ISBN 9781443133708 (hardcover)
Classification: LCC PS8595.I834 A63 2019 | DDC jC813/.54—dc23

www.scholastic.ca

Author photo by: David Shuken.

6 5 4 3 2 1   Printed in Malaysia 108   19 20 21 22 23 24

For Anne Shone, who sparkles.
　　　　　　　　　　　　— F.W.

*For my boy Jake, for sitting faithfully
under my desk, waiting until our next
run in the park.*
　　　　　　　　　　　　— E.P.

My friend Alfie always gets dirty.

He jumps in puddles.
He dives in leaves.
He rolls in sand.

Alfie tries to stay clean.

He didn't mean
to knock over
the oatmeal this
morning.

He didn't mean to
knock over the milk.

He didn't mean to get blueberry jam all over his face.

Alfie,
no!

Alfie just likes to explore. He was sure there was treasure in the barn.

He only wanted to see where the rabbit lived.

He was sure he could
dig up a dinosaur.

Alfie likes to play.
He thought the chickens liked tag too.
He only wanted to say hi to the pigs.
He didn't want to fall in the mud.

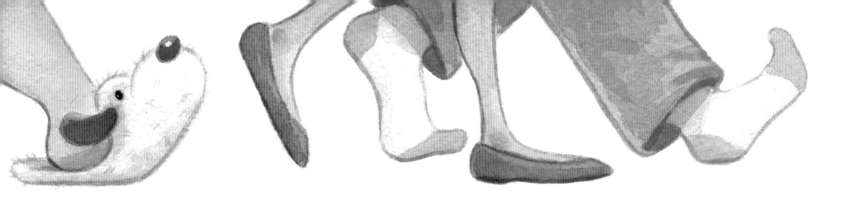

Yes! Yes! Yes!

But Alfie didn't want to listen.

Come on, Alfie!
Jump into the bath with me.

Alfie blew giant bubbles.
Alfie made giant splashes.

Alfie got wet all over.

Ta-da! Alfie sparkles!

And Rufus,
you sparkle too!